KU-609-512

This book belongs to:

_____

A catalogue record for this book is available from the British Library

Published by Ladybird Books Ltd Loughborough Leicestershire UK
Ladybird Books is a subsidiary of the Penguin Group of companies

Text and illustrations © Lesley Harker MCMXCV
© LADYBIRD BOOKS LTD MCMXCV
This edition MCMXCVI
LADYBIRD and the device of a Ladybird are trademarks of Ladybird Books Ltd

Wishing Moon

by Lesley Harker

Ladybird

Persephone Brown was tired of being small. "All I see are feet and knees. I wish I had a pair of stilts," she said, "or a tall giraffe to ride on."

When she went shopping,
she only saw the lowest shelves.

And when she went to the woods,
she could only reach the lowest branches.

And when she went to Grandma's house, she couldn't even reach the doorknocker!

When it was Christmas,
Persephone Brown asked
Father Christmas for a ladder.

And for her birthday she wanted a flying trapeze.

"Mum," said Persephone, "I'm sick of being small."

"You'll soon grow," said her mum. "Eat your beans, Persephone."

Persephone Brown went into the garden. (She had to ask her mother to open the back door.)

"I HATE BEING SMALL!" she yelled, "I WANT TO BE BIG!"

Because that night it was a Wishing Moon, she got her heart's desire.

All of a sudden Persephone Brown was HUGE! So huge, she couldn't fit in the house. She had to live in the garden.

When she stood up she banged her head on the tree-tops. And when she sat down she squashed all the rhubarb!

But worst of all she couldn't get into her new red wellies.

"OUCH!" said Persephone, "OUCH! OUCH! BOTHER!"

"Mum," shouted Persephone down the chimney, "I'm tired of being tall."

"Never mind," said her mother, "I expect you'll get used to it. Could you just give the upstairs windows a wipe, dear?"

Persephone Brown yelled up at the Moon, "I've changed my mind," she said, "I wish I was small again."

The Moon tut-tutted to itself. "Some people are never satisfied!"

"Well, I'm sorry," explained Persephone, "but I didn't know being big would be so difficult."

"I'm big," said the Moon, huffily, "I don't find it difficult at all."

"But you don't have to shout at your mum down a chimney," said Persephone. "I don't even fit in my house anymore."

"Never mind, you know fresh air is much better for you," said the Moon. "It builds up your muscles and puts colour in your cheeks."

"But what about my Grandma?" said Persephone. "Now she's old she doesn't see so well. I'm too far away up here."

"Can't you buy her a telescope?" muttered the Moon.

"No!" said Persephone Brown.

"Well, at least you can reach her doorknocker now," said the Moon.

"Only if I bend right down and get a crick in my neck!" said Persephone.

"I haven't heard one good reason to change you back again yet," said the Moon to Persephone Brown.

"Because I want my mum to give me a big cuddle and tuck me up in my bed like she used to," she said.

The Moon smiled. "Well, of course you do," it said, "and that IS the very best reason I ever heard. You get your wish, Persephone Brown..."

And...

WHOOSH down she went like a popped balloon!

KNOCK! KNOCK! went
Persephone on the front door.

"Who's there?" said Mum.

"Someone just the right size!"
said Persephone Brown.

"Goodnight, Wishing Moon."